Daniel
the
Draw-er

S. J. Henderson

Daniel the Draw-er

This book is a work of fiction. Any similarities to real people, living or dead, is purely coincidental, but, admit it, would be kind of awesome. All characters and events in this work are figments of the author's imagination. Especially the four-eyed aliens from the planet Beezo.

Special thanks to Courtney, Brad, Cody, Tim, Mandy, Sky Writers, Story Cartel, and the Author of all things.

To Gram, Sydney, Mr. Big, Princess,
Ella, Samantha, Owen, Lucy, Zoe,
Addie, Koen, Saige, and Katelyn.

And, of course—

Logan, William Hunter, Ethan, and
Isaac.

There's magic inside each and every
one of us.

. . . Pancakes.

Chapter 1

"Did you make any new friends at school today?" Mom asks, smiling at me as she wipes crumbs from the counter. Every day it's the same question, and every day I give the same answer. They say adults are supposed to be smart, but maybe no one told Mom.

I grab the carton of milk and take a gulp before she notices, then wipe away my milk moustache with my sleeve. Today I feel dramatic, so I puff up my chest and place my hands on my hips like a superhero before booming, "Annie is the only friend I need!"

If I owned a cape I would make sure it flapped in the breeze behind me the whole time, but capes weren't on the shopping list for school clothes this year. Mom looks disappointed. I'm disappointed, too. Capes are cool. Not as cool as samurai swords or skateboarding dogs, but still pretty awesome.

"Daniel. Annie is a nice girl, but it's not healthy to have only one friend."

Parents always say stuff isn't healthy for you. Candy bars aren't healthy. Staying up all night watching television isn't healthy. Now being friends with Annie isn't healthy. Unless Mom means the time Annie sneezed right in my face and I ended up sick in bed for two days,

I don't understand how having Annie as my friend can be bad.

"Really, Daniel. What if Annie moved away? Then you wouldn't have any friends."

"She's not going anywhere. She told me so."

Her face grows serious. "Promise me you'll at least *try* to talk to the other kids."

"Yeah, yeah." I roll my eyes, but make sure I turn my back to her first. Mom hates it when I roll my eyes. Only she can roll her eyes and get away with it. "What's for dinner?"

"Meatloaf, your favorite."

Gross! I stick out my tongue and make a gagging noise.

"I was going to warn you that Tommy's in the living room waiting for your sister, but since you're being a smarty-pants, maybe I won't . . ."

Tommy. Ugh.

My sister Lila's latest boyfriend, Tommy, is the worst one yet. He plays in a band and has just enough hair on his chin to make it look like he's super-glued a caterpillar there. Tommy also likes to call me "buddy" and punch me in the arm. I figure he can't remember my name. When we first met, Tommy called me Fritz for an entire day before Lila finally put a stop to it.

* * * *

I tiptoe down the hall past the living room door, but knock into the coat rack with my backpack. Like a hungry lion, Tommy pounces, jumping over the back of the couch and directly in front of me. *Great.*

"Bud-dy!" He punches me in the arm, as always.

"Ow," I whine. Before he can hit me again, I slip off my backpack and hide my arms behind it like a knight with a shield.

"What's up, big guy?"

I try to answer him, but it's kind of hard since he's put me in a headlock, his skinny forearm pressing into my windpipe. Up close, Tommy smells like microwave burritos and cat litter. He rubs his knuckles on the top of my head and I yelp. When the torture portion of our meeting ends, he lets me go and acts like nothing ever happened.

"Lila says you're a draw-er."

I'm pretty sure he means *artist*, but my head and arm still hurt so I keep my mouth shut.

"Uh, I guess so." I shrug.

Tommy smiles, making the caterpillar wiggle. "Well, keep practicing, buddy. Maybe if you get good enough you can draw a cover for *Revenge of the Lunch Lady*."

I back around him so I can keep an eye on his hands. "Yeah, okay. Thanks." *Like that'll happen.*

Revenge of the Lunch Lady is the name of Tommy's band, and their biggest show so far had been at the bowling alley. No one had been able to hear them over the thumps of bowling balls and crash of falling pins. That's probably for the best.

The rest of the way to my room, I think about Mom's words, *What if Annie moved away?*

It's impossible to imagine life without my best friend. While all the other girls at school dress in pink and smell like flowers, Annie always smells like peanut butter and wears her brother's old jeans. Back in kindergarten she ate an earthworm and that's when I knew she was the one.

The other kids tease us and say we're going to get married when we grow up. They make kissy noises when we walk past together, but that's gross. I don't want to kiss Annie. Annie eats earthworms, after all.

Mom's being silly. Annie's not leaving.

Once I reach my room, I sit down at my table and get to work. Dad put my table in front of the window so I can look out and draw nice pictures of trees and birds, but mostly I use the window as a launch pad for paper airplanes and plastic parachute men. Instead of trees and birds, I draw a lot of animals and super-awesome machines nobody else has thought of yet. My favorite is a robot named Pi-zzabot that can bake a pizza and do my Math homework at the same time. I drew a toaster that can tie shoes and smear peanut butter on bread for Annie, too, but I still think Pi-zzabot is better.

Today I want to finish the animal I've been working on for a few days. I mean, I *guess* he's an animal. His head is round and soft like a teddy bear, with shiny black eyes, but he's no ordinary teddy bear. Once I finish, the rest of his body will have long tentacles like an octopus. It's going to be awesome.

In the middle of drawing Octobear's third oozing tentacle, my pencil lead snaps off. I growl and fling my wounded pencil out the open window before I realize that was my only pencil.

* * * *

Lila's in her room with her door open when I stomp by. She leans in close to the mirror on her dresser and dabs at her eyelashes with a tiny black brush. Girls are weird. You'd never catch me poking myself in the eye with anything to look pretty.

I poke my head into her room. "Hey, you got a pencil?"

She stops and looks at me with the brush hovering near her eyeball. I flinch and look away. Just because Lila is my sister doesn't mean I want her to become a cyclops or wear a patch over her eye.

"No, Daniel," she replies. "I do not *have* a pencil."

Who died and made her an English teacher all of the sudden? She probably needs to help poor Tommy out, not me, since he can't even come up with a better word than "draw-er." I stalk away, taking back all the nice things I'd ever said about her, which weren't that many.

I want to ask Mom about pencils, but Tommy and his fists still lurk in the living room. Octobear needs more legs, but if Tommy punches me one more time my arm's going to fall off. Without my arm, it'll be hard to draw.

The only other place to look is the attic. I'm not supposed to snoop around up there because Mom says I make a mess. This one time I found a bunch of brand new action figures Dad hadn't even opened yet. His face turned purple when he found me playing with them a few days later. Since then, the attic has been off-limits for me. Octobear needs me, though.

It takes a while, but I find a box of old art supplies buried under a fake Christmas tree and a bin of my old baby clothes. The stuff inside the box is mostly junk. I push aside a stack of paper with brown water spots and small containers of dried-up paint until I feel something smooth and wooden. The wooden thing ends up being a case, and when I open it there's a half-used pencil wrapped in green velvet. *Yes!* Why anyone would put a plain old pencil in a box like that, I don't know, but Dad is weird and keeps his toys in boxes, too. With a shrug, I toss the cardboard box to the side and hurry back down to my room.

* * * *

I finish drawing the last of Octobear's limbs and start on a cat who will have a jetpack on his back when Mom calls me down for dinner. The meatloaf is extra dry tonight and Dad talks for a whole ten minutes about some market on Wall Street, wherever that is. As soon as I choke down the last awful bite, I run back to my room, ready to send a cat into orbit.

Only one problem: there's a cat on my desk and he looks kind of familiar.

The cat stands up and puffs his snowy fur. "Hey, pal," he says.

I rub my eyes then look over my shoulder towards the stairs where the rest of my family is still talking about James Bond or something. I knew this day would come—Mom's meatloaf has finally driven me insane.

"Not gonna answer me?" He closes his yellow eyes and shakes his head. "That's fine. But do me a favor, kid?"

My mouth hangs open. I try to speak but the words get stuck inside of me.

He turns to the paper lying on the desk next to him and I see an empty space where his back should be. With his paw, he pats my cat drawing on the page.

"Finish drawing me."

I slam the door behind me and run downstairs as fast as I can. Mom said she wanted me to make new friends, and now I guess I have.

Chapter 2

I beg my parents, who are clearing off the dining room table, to let me sleep in their bedroom.

Dad doesn't even look at me before saying no.

"But . . . I had a bad dream."

Mom puts her hands on her hips. "Daniel, you have to go to sleep before you can have nightmares."

Oh, yeah.

This calls for drastic measures, the one thing I know Mom can't resist. I'm not proud of what I'm about to do, but there's a fake cat in my room.

My lip wobbles.

"No way," Dad says, more to Mom than me. "I've got an important meeting tomorrow and I've got to sleep."

My eyes meet his and I give him a look that tells him *I'll remember that.* Never mind him. We both know Mom's the one in charge.

I whimper and flutter my eyelashes at Mom. "Pwwwwwease?"

She sighs. "Okay. But go change into your PJs."

She wants me to change into my pajamas, which are in my dresser in my room. The same room where I've locked up a white cat who should be a drawing on a piece of paper. *I don't think so.*

While they finish with the dishes, I curl up in the middle of their bed still wearing my jeans and t-shirt. If I fall asleep before they come to bed, they won't make me change. And if they don't make me change, I won't have to see that freaky cat again. It's not a very good plan, but what do you expect? I'm only nine.

* * * *

Morning sunlight streams in through the window. I blink a few times and try to remember where I am. Since when did my parents have a Godzilla poster on their wall, a poster a lot like the one in my room? I stare up at glow-in-the-dark stars just like the ones on my bedroom ceiling. And when did we get a cat?

A cat!

I jump back as far away as I can get from the white cat sitting at the foot of my bed. Dad must have carried me down here in the middle of the night. He's officially my least favorite parent. I plan to tell him so, if I make it out of this alive.

The cat's tail twitches against my comforter. "Relax, kid. I'm not going to hurt you."

"Y-y-y-you . . . talk?" I blurt out.

"So do you. I wondered there, for a minute." The cat swipes at his nose with his paw. "Sorry. That was rude. The name's—"

"Whiskers."

"—Whiskers." He finishes.

I know his name already because that's the name I'd given to my cat drawing.

"But where did you—? How did—?"

The cat hops down from my bed, to the floor, up to my chair, and then to my desk where the drawing and pencil lay. He picks the pencil up in his mouth and leaps through the air until he's back on the bed.

"Dittth penthhhil itth nuh uhhdinanee penthhhil," he explains.

I wrinkle up my nose. "Huh?"

"Oh, thoweee." He lets the pencil drop from his mouth. "I *said*, this pencil is no ordinary pencil. It's magic."

Funny, the pencil looks plain enough to me, with its yellow paint, band of metal, and worn pink eraser.

"The magic brings the drawings to life."

But if that's true, then Octobear should be around here somewhere. I remember finishing him up before dinner last night, before I'd started on

Whiskers. I lean over the side of the bed, my head nearly touching the ground, and peek into the darkness.

The cat watches me with his head cocked to the side. "If you're looking for the bear thing, I'll save you the trouble." He jumps to the ground and trots to the far side of my desk. A few seconds later, he returns with something hanging from his mouth. It's floppy and covered in spots that look like little suction cups. Green slime trails from the tip.

"What did you do to him?" The idea of him chowing down on Octobear makes me sick to my stomach.

Whiskers, who is scrubbing the slime from his tongue with a paw, stops. "I didn't do anything. You only drew part of him with the magic pencil, remember? Besides, I hate sushi."

Sure enough, the other three tentacles lay in an oozing heap on my floor. The rest of Octobear is nowhere to be found.

"Oh, hey," Whiskers says. "That reminds me. You got any food in this place? I'm starving."

I leave him in my room and head to the kitchen in search of something he might like. The only thing I find is a hunk of last night's meatloaf, which I bring to him cold since I've been banned from using the microwave. Set fire to *one kitchen* and everyone freaks out.

Whiskers buries his nose in the meatloaf. After a good whiff, he arches the spot where his back should be and hisses at the blob of mystery meat on the plate. "I thought you were going to bring me *food*," he complains.

"Sorry," I say. "I can bring you better stuff after school."

Whiskers grunts and turns his back to me so I can change my clothes.

* * * *

All day long during school, I imagine all the cool things I'll draw when I get home and back to the magic pencil. My teacher, Mrs. Konkle, calls on me twice during Math class and I don't know the answer either time. A couple of kids laugh at me and my face feels hot. If Pi-zzabot was real, he could give me the right answers, plus I wouldn't have to eat the bologna sandwich Mom packed in my lunch.

Pi-zzabot! Yes! That's what I'll draw.

I'm so excited about Pi-zzabot, I doodle him on the edge of the paper I'm supposed to be using for long division. Mrs. Konkle stops next to my desk just as I put the finishing touch on the oven in Pi-zzabot's stomach. She taps my desk with her fingers and I jump. I try to cover Pi-zzabot with my hand, but it's too late.

"That doesn't look like Math."

"Pi-zzabot already knows how to divide. He doesn't need to practice." *And since Pi-zzabot will be doing my Math homework from now on, I don't need to practice either.* But I don't tell Mrs. Konkle that.

The corners of her mouth twitch like she wants to smile, but all she says is, "Put it away, Daniel."

* * * *

At lunch, Annie sits down next to me and pulls her sandwich from her lunchbox. She pumps her fist. "Yes! Peanut butter and jelly."

Annie's mom always packs her peanut butter sandwiches. One time she sent a tuna fish sandwich instead. Annie spent the whole lunch period searching for a kid who would trade their peanut butter and jelly sandwich for her tuna fish. She ended up really hungry that day.

"My dad set up the tent in the backyard yesterday. Wanna come over after school and play Army?" Her mouth is full of mashed-up food when she talks. She does that on purpose to gross me out. I chew up my bite of bologna sandwich and stick out my tongue.

"That's disgusting." Annie laughs. I like her laugh. It's high and squeaky like a chipmunk.

"Nah," I say. "I can't today." I know I should tell her about my big plan to bring Pi-zzabot to life, but I'm not ready. The weird pencil is my secret, and I'm not ready to tell anyone about it, not even my best friend.

Her smile fades, but I'm too busy dreaming about pizza and freedom from homework to notice.

Chapter 3

"Hi, sweetie," Mom says when I get home from school. She's at the counter chopping lettuce with a big knife. I usually complain when she calls me 'sweetie,' but today I'll let it slide.

She stops chopping long enough to ask, "Did you make any new friends at school today?"

I don't answer her because I'm already halfway down the hall.

* * * *

Tommy scares me nearly to death when he jumps in front of me.

"Hey, buddy." The caterpillar on his chin stretches into the letter "U" when he smiles. I'm distracted long enough to forget he's about to punch me.

"Armadillo!" I yell when he hits me. It's the first thing I think of, because an armadillo can roll up into a little ball when it's being attacked. Being an armadillo sure would save me from a lot of bruises.

Tommy scrunches up his face. "Wait . . . What did you just call me?"

"Nothing. Never mind," I mumble, and walk by him before he can punch me for real.

* * * *

When I open my door, my room is empty. I wonder if Mom found Whiskers while I was at school and threw him outside. Maybe Whiskers didn't really exist and had only been a nightmare, thanks to Mom's meatloaf.

But it wasn't a nightmare. The plate of cold meatloaf I'd brought him this morning still sits on the end of my bed. Whiskers left a few bites behind, and they are now dried up like little rocks. Gross little rocks.

Maybe Whiskers went outside. What would an imaginary-but-real talking cat with no back do outside? Chase mice? Talk to other talking cats? I don't even know the basic stuff like if he has claws or if he needs a litter box. Maybe he wandered outside to go potty or file his nails and got lost.

Losing Whiskers makes my insides feel heavy. We've never had a pet before because Lila's allergic to everything. Well, we had a fish once, but he didn't last very long. After about two weeks I found Mr. Bloop sleeping in his tank upside down. When I got home from school, Mr. Bloop, his tank—*everything*—was gone. I guess Mom didn't like having a fish that took naps.

I close the door behind me and look around. No Whiskers. I kneel down and peek under my bed. There are three balled-up socks, an old notepad, and a few toy cars, but still no Whiskers.

"Whiskers," I call out. My voice shakes. There's no trace of the white cat, and I don't know whether to be happy he's gone or sad because talking cats are definitely cooler than capes.

I decide to sit down at the desk and pull out my drawing paper and start on Pi-zzabot to keep myself from worrying about Whiskers. Since I spent a lot of time at school practicing, it doesn't take me long to sketch the robot out on a new piece of paper with the magic pencil.

My stomach growls. I can almost taste the pizza from my awesome invention. *I'll never have to eat another bite of meatloaf, ever!*

I'm connecting the last line on my drawing when something smacks against my window. And again. Outside, hugging his body around a branch of the tree that hangs close to the side of the house, is Whiskers.

I pull the window open. "How did you get out there?"

"I-I-I was b-b-bored." The words chatter from his mouth. Whiskers trembles and the branch shakes under him. "I'm n-n-n-not bored anymore!"

"Well, c'mon in, then." I move away from the window to give him room.

He pinches his golden eyes shut. "Can't."

"Why not? Just jump in here."

Whiskers moves his head only a little, from side to side. He tries not to make big motions because the tree makes big motions, too.

"Afraid. Of heights."

The branch is too far away for me to reach Whiskers and pull him inside, so I'll have to think of some other way to help.

There's not much in my room to help him, unless I tie my sheets together like they did in that one movie where the bank robbers tried to escape from the prison. If Whiskers had thumbs, that might work. But Whiskers does not have thumbs, and the bad guys on the movie fell trying to escape and ended up back in jail.

Whiskers, Whiskers, Whiskers . . . Whiskers in a tree. Whiskers in the air. How can I get the scared kitty from the tree to my room? It's too bad cats can't fly. If Whiskers could fly, he could chase birds through the sky then zoom right in through my window. I think of the empty space on his back and snap my fingers.

Flying cats! Yes!

The drawing of Whiskers sits on the corner of my desk still waiting for me to finish. I scribble something on the page and then I wait for something to happen.

And wait.

I'm not sure how my drawings become real.

"Abracadabra! Alakazam!" I shout. Nothing happens. Whiskers looks like he's getting more pale, but it's hard to tell since he's already white.

"Presto chango!"

Behind me, something clanks and beeps.

"Pi-zzabot at your service," says the robot. "How may I help you, sir?"

With all of the excitement of trying to keep Whiskers from falling out of the tree and finding out exactly how many lives a cat has, I'd forgotten about drawing the robot. I smile.

"Pi-zzabot, I'd like you to help Whiskers."

The robot marches up to the window, making a ton of noise. I should have drawn his legs with knee joints instead of straight metal tubes. I'll have to fix that next time I draw him.

Pi-zzabot scans the tree then looks back at me. "Sir, *whom* do you wish me to serve?"

"Whiskers," I say. I point at the cat.

"What would you like on your pizza, Mr. Whiskers?"

"No, Pi-zzabot! He's not hungry."

Pi-zzabot tips his metal head in shame. "My apologies. Do you need help with your Math homework, Mr. Whiskers?"

This isn't going to work. Pi-zzabot was designed for two things and only two things: Math and pizza. Saving Whiskers isn't Math or pizza.

Whisker's back paws slip on the bark and he scrambles to keep his balance. I look back at the paper and what I've just drawn. It hasn't shown up yet and I'm afraid Whiskers will be one life less before it does.

This is the slowest magic I've ever used. It's the only magic I've ever used, of course, but it's also the slowest.

There was an old show on television once where a cat was stuck up in a tree and the little old lady called the fire department to come rescue it. I am pretty sure firemen have better things to do with their time than climbing trees and getting clawed by cats, even in the olden days, but I am all out of ideas.

I head towards the telephone and make it halfway down the hallway before I hear a thud. When I run back into my room, Pi-zzabot smiles at me with his mouth made out of a sequence of little red lights. "How may I help you, sir?"

He's only trying to help, but I ignore him. Whiskers is under my bed. The jet pack sputters little puffs of smoke before orange flames spring to life.

"Get this thing off of me," Whiskers cries as the rocket sends him straight up to the ceiling.

"How may I help you, Mr. Whiskers?" the robot beeps.

"Unless . . . you can . . . make me a . . . pizza with . . . the magic eraser, then . . . you *can't*." The cat bounces off of stuff like he's the ball inside a pinball machine.

Pi-zzabot makes a series of beeping noises as he thinks about this request. For a robot, he's not very smart.

"I'm sorry, sir. I do not know what 'magic eraser' is. Would you like anchovies instead?"

"Why do you think I like anchovies? Because I'm a cat?" Whiskers looks upset by this for a moment, and then he ends up head-first in my wastebasket.

"Wait," I say. "Magic eraser? What magic eraser?"

The wastebasket muffles his voice. "The one on the end of the pencil. *Duh!*"

"Hold on," I cry as Whiskers and the wastebasket shoot across the floor. I bring the tip of the eraser to the drawing and begin scrubbing away at it.

"Thank . . ." The rocket flares and Whiskers is in the air. He lands on my ceiling fan, which starts spinning. "Goo-oo-oo-oo . . . GOODNESS! HELP!"

Though it takes only seconds to erase the jet pack and a few seconds more for it to finally disappear, it's long enough for Whiskers to lose his grip on the fan and land upside down on my floor with a surprised "meow." He rolls over to sitting and rubs the side of his head with his paw.

I kneel down next to him. "Are you okay?"

"A jet pack? Seriously, Daniel? Next time you decide to strap me to a rocket, at least draw me a helmet, too," he grumbles. "And in case you wondered, I am afraid of heights. But now I'm more afraid of flying."

So much for flying cats. After that, Whiskers asks me to never, ever give him a jet pack again, and to draw something better instead: a straight line.

Chapter 4

Every Saturday is "Annie and Daniel" day. As soon as Annie finishes her breakfast (peanut butter on toast, what else?) she rides her bike the three blocks between our houses and we spend the whole day playing.

I used to ride to her house but I outgrew my bike over the summer. My parents said I have to use Lila's old bike until my birthday in March. Lila's bike is hot pink and silver streamers dangle from the handles. There's even a big white basket on the front. I'd rather walk barefoot over a pit of snapping turtles than be seen riding around on the Princessmobile.

Annie's bike is blue, just plain blue, with no streamers or anything. I tried to talk her into trading bikes once. She laughed her chipmunk laugh and pedaled away. Now Annie comes to my house instead so I don't have to listen to the other kids call me "Danielle" while I ride down the street.

I'm busy drawing a pile of coins and eating a bowl of Yummy-O's at my desk when Dad pops his head into my room.

"Annie's here," he says through a sip of coffee. It sounds like he's underwater, talking and snorkeling at the same time. Snorkeling coffee sounds painful.

There's a scurrying, scratching noise under my bed. Whiskers ran under there to hide amongst the socks and lost Army men.

"What have I told you about food in your room, Daniel? The mice will get in here." Dad wrinkles his nose and bends down to check under the bed.

"No!" I jump out of my chair before he can spot my fluffy friend. "I mean . . . I won't do it again, I promise."

He stands back up and sips his coffee. "Good. Now, go get Annie before she breaks something."

Poor Annie. Shatter one lamp, two picture frames, and a glass paperweight and no one lets you forget it. Ever. In her defense, that butterfly did look like it was up to no good.

I look over my shoulder one last time at my magic pencil and my notepad and sigh. Becoming crazy rich will have to wait for a few more minutes.

* * * *

Annie meets me at the front door still wearing her backpack. Something long and skinny sticks out from a gap in the zipper.

"I saved up my allowance and bought a marshmallow shooter." She grins, showing off the space where her front teeth still haven't grown back in. "And two bags of ammo. Let's go. "

A marshmallow shooter! I've wanted one of those for as long as I can remember. Every time I ask for one, Mom says they're too violent. No one in the history of time has ever marshmallowed to death, but Mom disagrees. She tells me marshmallows are meant for the middle of S'mores, not the middle of a battle. Mom's no fun.

Now Annie has a marshmallow shooter and I don't. Maybe she'll share, giving me short turns to her long ones. Somehow I get the feeling that I'll spend most of the day as Annie's moving target instead of actually getting a turn. We were supposed to buy our marshmallow shooters at the same time so we could both have fun at the same time.

Maybe I can still get my own marshmallow shooter. Mom never said I couldn't buy a shooter with my own money, only that *she* wouldn't buy me one. Lucky for me, I know of a pile of cold, hard cash that should already be waiting in my room, ready to be spent on candy, video games, and junk-food-hurling weapons. I dash down the hallway, leaving Annie by the front door.

* * * *

Stacks of gold coins spill over on the floor next to my desk. I drop to my knees in front of the money pile. "I'm rich! I'm rich!" I yell as I pick up handfuls of treasure and toss them into the air.

But they feel wrong. They're too light and crinkly in my fingers. I place one in my teeth and bite down like I've seen them do in old movies, which is supposed to tell me something. It tells me something, all right. Silver foil and chocolate fill my mouth.

Chocolate! My fortune won't buy me anything except a tummy ache.

Annie plops down on my bed. "Dude! Where did you get all the candy? Can I have some?"

"Whatever." I toss a few coins to Annie as I turn to study my drawing. She wasn't ready to catch them and I hear one roll across the floor.

I don't understand why the magic pencil didn't work this time. For once in my life, I hadn't been thinking of candy. Maybe if I had drawn dollar bills instead of coins then they would have . . .

Annie's muffled voice interrupts my thoughts. "Hey. What's this?"

"What's *what*?" I ask, looking up from my notebook. She's on her hands and knees, peeking under my bed. *Whiskers* is under the bed. My heart starts pounding and I feel like I'm going to be sick. Eventually I planned on telling Annie about the magic pencil. Really. But I thought eventually would be more like next week.

"The cat! Under your bed," Annie squeals.

Whiskers is plastered against the far wall but his eyes give him away. They shine like a glow stick even in the shadows.

"Uh, meow?" Whiskers offers.

"What's wrong with your cat? He sounds weird."

Whiskers blinks twice. "What's wrong with *me*? How would you like it if I asked Daniel, here, what's wrong with you?" He looks at me. "Hey, Daniel. How come your friend smells like she's been eating dirt?"

"Hey!" Annie says. "I have not!" Then she realizes she's arguing with a cat and scrambles to her feet.

"Wait, Annie," I say.

She backs up to the door, not taking her eyes from the floor by my bed. Her face is the same strange shade of green as the slime from Octobear's tentacles. "He . . . ? What . . . ? I don't . . . ?"

"That's Whiskers. He's magic."

"Magic?" she croaks.

"I drew him. With this." I hold out the magic pencil.

"Daniel, I'm going home. I think I'm having a nightmare. Or a fever. Or . . ." Annie scoots out the bedroom and down the hallway.

"You're not sick. Whatever I draw with this pencil comes to life." *Well, except for my pile of money.*

She pretends not to hear me and keeps walking.

"Stop!" I rush past her and block the front door. "I can prove it. Let me grab my notebook and I'll let you draw anything you want."

* * * *

Twenty minutes later we're in the woods behind my house. A pale pink unicorn with a long purple mane stares us down. Despite its girly color scheme, the horn on its forehead looks sharp enough to poke holes through me.

"A pink unicorn? That's your favorite animal?"

She shrugs and takes a step forward to pet the unicorn's shoulder. "Don't you dare tell anyone about Macaroni."

Annie has a certain reputation to keep, one that involves a taste for creepy-crawly and peanut-buttery things. If anyone besides me found out there's an actual girl hidden inside, she'd never live it down. Neither of us can handle any more kissy noises in the hallway at school, so her secret's definitely safe with me.

I shrug. "Hey, I won't tell anyone your favorite animal if you won't tell anyone about the pencil."

"It's a deal. Now draw your stuff already so we can play."

While Annie practices riding Macaroni around the trees, I get to work drawing. It takes a while, but soon everything's there:

A blue dragon named Herman who can fly.

Four-eyed aliens from the planet Beezo.

And my very own marshmallow shooter.

Chapter 5

Four-eyed aliens from Beezo like pizza. We find that out on accident when Pizzabot clanks out into the woods to ask me if I'm hungry or if I need to know the square root of nine.

The tallest of the aliens spots him first. "Bzzip zoop zup. Bzzzerp fwam moo."

He said moo.

Moo.

I laugh and nudge Annie with my elbow. She's not laughing.

"Uh, he's got a . . ."

The leader of the aliens pulls some kind of gun from the belt around his waist, and the other five green guys do the same. They point their weapons at Pi-zzabot, whose red-dot mouth lights up in a smile.

"Bzzap pinch . . . GOO!"

"Did he just say he wanted to pinch goo?" Annie asks with a shaking voice.

Before I can answer her, the aliens fire. Streams of bubbles pour from the ends of their guns and float through the air.

I look at Annie. Her mouth hangs open.

The aliens look confused, too. All four of the tall one's eyes close for a second, and then he raises his gun again.

"Bzzap pinch . . . GOO!" He orders.

Again, they shoot bubbles at Pi-zzabot. Pi-zzabot keeps grinning his electronic grin.

The alien leader nods his head at one of the others in his group. With a gulp, the smallest four-eyed alien steps toward Pi-zzabot. He shuffles a few feet forward, looks back at his friends one last time, then stretches his webbed hand out in front of him. It feels like it takes his fingers—or maybe they call them bzzingers or something—a million years before they collide with Pi-zzabot with a "ping." The little alien whimpers and jumps back, firing his bubble gun right in Pi-zzabot's face.

"What would you like on your pizza, Mr. Extraterrestrial Being?" Pi-zzabot asks as the bubbles clear from around his head.

The alien scrambles backward to his group. "Bzzzay kong pan."

"Excellent, sir. I'll have your bacon and ham pizza in just a moment," the robot says as his insides begin to whir.

The big alien barks something at the smaller one then punches him in the arm. The little one frowns and rubs his arm with his hand. I know how he feels. Even aliens have Tommys, I guess.

Soon the pizza is done and Pi-zzabot holds it out to the group of green creatures. They won't touch it, of course, and shower him with bubbles again.

This is silly.

"Guys, I . . . come in peace," I say, because that's what you say to aliens. Twenty-four eyes blink back with guns ready to bubble me. The pizza looks good and it's going to go to waste, so I grab a piece for me and one for Annie. We eat it while the aliens watch.

"So good," Annie says with her mouth full. "But it kind of tastes like soap."

When we finish our pizza, I look the small alien in two of his eyes and point at the rest of the pizza on Pi-zzabot's tray. He glances at the others, then snatches a piece and stuffs the entire thing in his mouth. And then he smiles and buzzes something to the rest of his group. The pizza disappears in seconds and Pi-zzabot has to make five more before the aliens stop chowing down.

* * * *

Four-eyed aliens also like S'mores, which we also find out by accident when we teach them how to play Army. While flying around on the back of Herman, my blue dragon, I shot a marshmallow at one of the aliens. Herman just happened to burp out a blast of flames at the right moment, and *POOF!* A golden brown marshmallow smacked my target right in his face. The alien used his snake-like forked tongue to wipe the goo from his cheek, then grinned, showing off three rows of silver teeth. Using Herman's fire and Macaroni's horn as a roasting stick, we went through the rest of our marshmallows, half of my pile of chocolate coins, and the rest of the graham crackers in the pantry until the aliens' bellies puffed out over their belts.

* * * *

Four-eyed aliens also like cats, which we find out when one of them spies Whiskers watching us from my window.

Eating a cat sounds like a quick way to give yourself a hairball, but I'm also not from a planet named Beezo. Before the drooling mob can climb the outside of my house and make an after-snack snack of my imaginary cat, Annie and I say good-bye. Soon all that's left of them is a pile of eraser shavings.

* * * *

My mom yells out the back door that it's time for dinner, which means it's time for Annie to go home. My mom used to let Annie eat dinner with us until she started sitting down at the table with our jar of peanut butter and a spoon instead of eating what the rest of us were having. Personally, I think Annie's a genius. If I didn't hate being grounded so much, I'd follow her lead.

Before I erase him, Annie gives Macaroni a kiss on his velvety nose. She keeps her back to me as the unicorn and my flying dragon disappear. I know she's trying to keep her crying a secret, but she can't stop snuffling. She takes a deep breath and wipes her nose on the back of her hand, then turns around.

"Sorry," I say. I don't know how to make her feel better. "We can draw Macaroni again next week." It'll take at least a week to clean up all of the Macaroni droppings, which seems like a lot of work for a magical creature. At least he didn't try to eat a household pet like the aliens or burn off anyone's eyebrows like Herman.

"Can I borrow the pencil tonight?" Annie asks.

"No," I snap without thinking.

"I'll bring it back in the morning, I promise."

"No!"

She stops walking. "Why not?"

"Because I said no, that's why." I sound exactly like my dad, except I can't put Annie in a 'Time Out' or give her a gross punishment like scrubbing toilets with a toothbrush.

"Please? I'll be really careful."

My hand tightens around the pencil. "It's *mine* and I don't have to share if I don't want to."

Her voice is quiet. "You're being mean, Daniel."

"And you're being greedy."

Annie blinks her wide eyes at me and doesn't say anything for a minute. Finally, she mutters, "See ya." She lifts her bike from where she dumped it in the grass this morning and pedals off without looking back.

Right away, my stomach swirls for the things I said. I hurt her feelings, and I don't know how to unhurt them. "Come over tomorrow, then," I yell after her. "We can draw Macaroni again."

"Why would you want to draw macaroni?" Tommy says as he walks down the front steps. Mom doesn't let Tommy eat dinner with us, either, because she hates it when he calls her "Mom." And because he burps every five seconds and doesn't say 'excuse me.' *When you gotta burp, you gotta burp*, I say, but I'm taking Mom's side for this one. At least until I'm big enough to defend myself against Tommy.

"Huh?"

"You're supposed to draw dinosaurs and monsters and stuff, not noodles."

He has no idea that I spent the last seven hours serving a buffet to visitors from another galaxy while riding on my very own dragon, or that the Macaroni I'm talking about could make him look like a slice of Swiss cheese. I'm too busy watching Annie and her streamer-free bike ride off into the sunset.

"You okay, buddy?" I almost think he's actually worried about me until he socks me in the arm and I drop my marshmallow shooter onto the driveway. If I had any marshmallows left I'd load it up and fire one off right in between his eyes, but the aliens cleaned me out. And now my marshmallow shooter lies in pieces on the driveway.

Chapter 6

Eighteen.

Eighteen is the number of pizzas it takes for me to get really, really sick of pizza.

And when I go back to school on Monday, Mrs. Konkle calls me up in front of the class to show off my perfect Math homework.

"Show them how you got your answer for number five, Daniel." She points to the chalkboard.

My shoes feel like they're full of bricks as I take my place at the board. I take a minute selecting the perfect piece of chalk. When I lift my hand to write the problem, I freeze as solid as an ice cube because I don't know the answer, Pi-zzabot does.

"I . . . Armadillo!" I say. It's the first word I think of because I want to curl up in a ball and die.

All of the other kids laugh at me, even Annie.

"Excuse me?" Mrs. Konkle says. She can't possibly know about my Math homework-doing robot, but she's smiling like a movie bad guy about ready to dangle the hero—me—above a pool of angry electric eels. She knows too much. Someone must stop her.

I ask to go to the school nurse because my stomach hurts *so bad*. The nurse makes me rest on a cot that smells like sweaty gym socks and bleach until my mom can pick me up from school. When Mom walks into the office, she pats my head and calls me "sweetie" (*ugh!*). As soon as we're outside, she turns into my real mom. "Alright, buster. I found all of the candy wrappers and pizza crusts in your room," she says. "Since you're *so* sick, I'm sure you won't mind spending the rest of the day sleeping."

My parents tell me that someday I will want to take naps all the time and I won't be able to, but *today* is not *someday*. I offer to let my Mom sleep while I stay up watching her recorded TV shows. She almost slams the brakes on in the middle of the road and turns right back around to the school. So I guess I'm taking a nap.

* * * *

Annie doesn't talk to me the whole next day. She even eats her peanut butter and jelly sandwich next to Pat Pratt in the lunchroom. Annie says she doesn't like Pat Pratt because he stepped on a frog on the playground two years ago. "Squishing frogs is cruel," says the girl who swallowed a worm whole.

Pat sees me and calls out, "Hey, wanna eat with us?"

I'm not sure he's talking to me, so I look over both of my shoulders just to be sure. No one's around, so I nod. "Thanks."

When I try to sit down next to her with my lunch, Annie says, "Someone's sitting here." Then she slides over to take up two spaces at the table so there isn't any room for me.

I end up by myself at the table with the broken bench, the one where you have to half-sit, half-stand unless you want to fall on your butt. On the bright side, my leg muscles should be pretty huge soon.

When I look over at Annie, her face is sad. Her mouth puckers like she ate something bad, and I wonder if she's gone back to eating earthworms. Then Frog-Squisher Pratt leans over and offers *my* best friend a cookie. Annie makes sure I'm watching as she gobbles up the whole thing. She tilts her head, and I can almost hear her squeak: *Frog-Squisher knows how to share with his friends, why don't you?*

Mom had warned me that someday Annie might go away. This is worse than Annie moving away, because Annie is still here. She just doesn't want anything to do with me.

* * * *

"Did you make any new friends at school today?" Mom asks later that afternoon. She's wearing rubber gloves and scooping the insides out of a raw chicken.

"Annie's the . . ." I gulp. "Oh, geez. Is that dinner?"

"Hush, Daniel!" Mom pretends she's going to throw a fistful of guts at me. I run from the kitchen with a yip, glad I don't have to talk to her about Annie.

I'm so busy running from the kitchen that I don't see him until it's too late. One second I'm dodging the threat of chicken missiles, the next I'm flat on the ground.

"Buddy!" Tommy says as he sticks his damp finger in my ear, the dreaded *wet willy.*

Tommy outweighs me by probably four times, and it's hard to breathe. Once I do take a breath, I wish I hadn't. Today he's wearing cheap cologne, the kind you can buy by the gallon at the drugstore, and it burns my nose and makes my eyes water. He lets me up after a few seconds, but I can tell that tomorrow I'm going to be sore from him crushing me like an empty soda can. If I could pick between arm punches and being tackled, I'd take the punches.

Later on, he tackles me again when I'm on my way to use the bathroom. I march back to my room, sit down with my notebook, and scribble so furiously my pencil could start a fire.

Whiskers joins me, plopping his fluffy behind on the edge of my desk. He runs his tongue over his paw. "So what's it gonna be today?"

"Tommy repellant," I growl.

He pauses. "Tommy *what*?" And then he looks down and shakes his head. "Oh no. Ohnonononono . . ."

"Maybe he'll leave me alone when he sees me walking around with this. And if he doesn't, then . . ."

The cat's back arches. "I've watched you draw some crazy things, Daniel, but this is a bad, bad idea."

"You worry too much," I say, finishing up the drawing. "It'll be fine."

But when the ferocious dog I'd drawn shows up in my room, it's not fine. He's a solid brick of muscle and bone, and his eyes are the color of blood.

Drool drips from his yellow teeth when he sees me.

"Uh-oh," I say.

The first thing the dog does is chase Whiskers straight out the window and onto the tree limb again. I crawl onto my desk and watch as he chews up my sneaker. When he's done with the shoe, he sniffs around and then pees on Pizzabot's leg.

"Daniel!" Whiskers yells. "Do something!"

"Yeah, yeah. I'm trying." I erase the vicious dog as fast as I can.

Honestly, I'm a little sad he won't get to pee on Tommy's leg.

The cat inches back down the branch, grumbling the whole time about how high off the ground he is. He closes his eyes and launches himself into the window. Once he stops shaking, he glares at me. "You gotta be more careful about what you draw, kid. Some things are just too scary or dangerous to bring to life. Like that octopus-bear thing you drew right before you drew me."

"Octobear?"

"Yeah, that thing. Did you know he has laser beams in his eyeballs?" Whiskers shudders. "Laser beams!"

Laser beams are way cooler than flying cats or capes, but Whiskers doesn't agree.

"He would slice us up with his lasers like a thick, juicy steak." He stops to lick his lips. "Speaking of steak, what's for dinner? If you say pizza again, I might have to find a new friend. Someone who eats steak, not pizza."

Whiskers is joking around, but he reminds me of my biggest problem.

No, not pizza.

I miss Annie.

Chapter 7

"So you're . . ."

"Super AmazingPants, at your service." The man throws his head back and sticks out his chest. The letters on his shirt spell S-A-P.

"Super . . . AmazingPants?"

"Thanks, but actually they're tights."

"No, no. I meant your name, Mr. Pants," I say.

He holds up his hand. "Please call me Sap. Mr. Pants is my father."

"Like the stuff that comes out of trees?" I ask, scratching my head. That's the weirdest superhero name I've ever heard. He's too busy flexing his muscles to reply.

We have the whole day off from school and I'm bored, and since Annie still acts like I'm invisible, I decided to draw a friend to play with. I started out drawing a boy my age with freckles and glasses, but then I erased him and drew Sap instead.

Usually when I draw something with the magic pencil I know what I'm making. As I draw, I give them names and think about things like what their favorite color is or if they have special powers. Not with Super Amazingpants.

I've always wanted a superhero for a friend. Sap, in person, isn't exactly what I'd imagined. Sure, he looks like a superhero, with slicked-back dark hair, gleaming teeth, and big muscles. He even wears his orange underpants on the outside, where there shouldn't be underpants. A bright orange cape hangs from his shoulders. At least *his* mom set some money aside for cool clothes.

"So, Sap," I say. "What do you want to do today?"

"Well, as you know, my nemesis, Doctor Short Shorts, is always up to no good."

"Your neme-what-sis?"

Sap laughs so loudly the windows shake. "My enemy. I'm good, he's bad. I'm chocolate chip cookies, he's . . ."

"Meatloaf?" I offer.

"Bingo!" he says. "Someone has to stop him from his crimes."

"Can I go with you?"

Sap rubs the dimple in his chin with his fingers as he thinks about my question. "Can you fly?"

"No. You can't carry me?"

He laughs again. "You watch too many movies. Do you know how hard it is to fly AND hold onto somebody? There's a reason more people don't travel by superhero."

I may not be able to fly, but I know someone who can. I snap my fingers and start scribbling on my notebook.

* * * *

A few minutes later I'm flying through the air on Herman's back. We learned the hard way that Sap's cape catches on fire easily, so he keeps some distance between himself and Herman's fire breath.

We're up so high in the clouds that I can't even see houses anymore, only squares of ground snapped together like puzzle pieces. After a while we pass a flock of geese flying in a big "V." We must look pretty strange because the goose in the back can't keep his eyes off us and ends up crashing into his neighbor.

"Ah-ha! Our first crime!" Sap yells above the wind. I thought he was talking about the goose accident, but his eyes are fixed on one of the puzzle pieces of earth below.

Together we dive through the clouds toward the ground, and my stomach flip-flops. I wonder what the crime will be: a bank robbery? A runaway train? A giant gorilla stuck at the top of a skyscraper? A surfing grizzly bear with a tommy gun and a score to settle?

Whatever it is, I hope there aren't any real guns because my mom would flip if she found out.

I'm also worried the bad guys won't know I'm a hero. At least Sap looks like a superhero in his yellow tights and orange cape, but I just look like me. I don't have any superpowers, either, unless you count my overactive imagination. I am riding a dragon, though. That has to count for something.

We land in the alley behind a grocery store, and I climb off Herman and let him waddle off to rest in the shade of the building. Sap presses his fingers to his forehead, using his Super Amazing vision to locate a way inside. It turns out his vision really isn't all that Super Amazing. The door leading inside is the size of a semi truck, standing wide open in the middle of the day, and I find it first.

"Eureka!" he booms when he reaches it.

I roll my eyes, then follow him into the dark building. We slip in between the mountains of cereal boxes and canned goods. A few workers walk past us without looking.

One guy stops and scrunches up his eyebrows. "Can I help ya, fellas?"

"No, good citizen. Just doing my job," Sap says. He doesn't even slow down. The man scratches his head and walks away.

We turn the corner into another room full of tall stacks of groceries still packed in boxes and plastic wrap. Sap stops so suddenly I run into him. "Suspect at two o'clock," he whispers.

"Two o'clock? But it's already almost five. I have to be home for dinner at—"

"No, Daniel. The criminal is RIGHT. THERE." He points off to the right where a guy is unpacking one of the boxes.

"Oh. Well, why didn't you say so?"

"I did," Sap sighs. "Follow me. Stay close—you never know where Dr. Short Shorts might strike next."

Together, we creep up to the man. He's whistling a song I've never heard before, and he looks a lot like my grandpa. I can't believe someone who looks like my grandpa could be a bad guy.

"Stop!" Sap's voice fills the huge room.

The old man jumps a little and places his hand on his heart. "Gee willikers! You scared me, boys."

Sap doesn't fall for the man's sweet and innocent act. He gets close enough to grab the man by the collar of his plaid shirt. "No! No! This is all wrong," he says.

"What are you doing?" the man sputters. "Get your hands off of me!"

"Plaids and stripes are an abomination," Sap says. "Who sent you?"

"Who what?"

"It was Dr. Short Shorts, wasn't it?" Sap demands.

I touch Sap on the elbow to stop him before he shakes the poor old man's head clear off his body. "He doesn't know. C'mon, let's go."

Sap blinks then lets go of the man. "Okay. But let this be a lesson to you. No plaids and stripes."

"No plaids and stripes," the man repeats as he backs away from us. As soon as he thinks he's far enough away, he turns and runs from the room.

Sap puts his hands on his hips and grins. "Victory is mine."

I have no idea what just happened.

"Uh, excuse me? What kind of evil do you fight, exactly?"

My question shocks him. "Why, crimes of fashion, of course."

Crimes of fashion. Of course.

* * * *

Before we head back to my house, we fight more crime:

A man at the bank wearing white tube socks and sandals.

A woman wearing pajama pants to pick up her dry cleaning.

A teenage boy at the music store wearing pants so tight I wonder if he can feel his toes.

An old lady wearing a bikini top and jean shorts to walk her dog.

And, together, Super AmazingPants and I help them all. None of the criminals will admit that Dr. Short Shorts is using them in his dastardly plan to take over the universe, but they don't have to. Anyone with eyes can see it's true.

* * * *

After dinner, I take Herman for one last spin with Sap before it's time to say good-bye. Spending time with a superhero, even a weird one obsessed with fashion, is cool but it's not the same as hanging out with Annie. She's funny and gross and doesn't care if I wear ugly rubber shoes or white after Labor Day or whatever.

I don't mean to fly over to Annie's house, it just happens because I'm thinking of her. It's starting to get dark out and light shines from Annie's second-story bedroom window. Once I'm sure Annie's not getting dressed, I fly Herman close to her window and throw acorns at the glass. At first she doesn't see us outside. She squints and moves close to the window until we're so close I could reach out and touch her. And then she screams.

"Shhh, Annie! It's just me and Herman." I try to quiet her down before her parents rush in and see me flying outside their daughter's bedroom on a blue dragon. That could get really weird.

"What in the world are you doing?" she asks once she quits screaming.

"Oh, you know . . . being superheroes and stuff." I shrug. "Wanna come with us?"

Annie stares at Sap. Sap stares at Annie. "Who's that guy?" she asks.

"Super AmazingPants," I say.

"Amazing . . . Pants?"

"Thanks." Sap smiles. "But they're more like tights."

She shakes her head. "I mean—"

Something rattles, and I look over in time to catch Sap working at Annie's window screen with his fingernails. "Dude, what are you doing?" I ask.

Sap tilts his head toward Annie. "Dr. Short Shorts is controlling this one, too. Check out those jeans."

"Sap! No!"

Annie bunches up her eyebrows and takes a step backward. "I think you should go home, Daniel. And Super Whateveryournameis."

I frown. "But I really wanted to—"

"Now," she says.

I talk Sap into leaving Annie alone, which isn't easy, but then he flies off into the sunset. Herman and I make one more loop around the block and then he drops me off at my front porch. A few minutes later, Herman disappears again. I don't erase Super AmazingPants, though. Someone's gotta be on the lookout for Dr. Short Shorts.

Chapter 8

Annie doesn't show up for this week's "Daniel and Annie" day. I try to make myself feel better by teaching Whiskers how to play Army. He doesn't have thumbs, though, so he keeps dropping the stick he's using as a gun. I ask him if he wants to use my new-and-improved marshmallow shooter, but he shakes his head. "I'm a lover, not a fighter," he says.

And then I hit him smack dab in the belly with a marshmallow.

"Mrrrrrrrrrrrrowwwww." He yowls and runs to hide behind the nearest tree.

He peeks his head out. "Tell me when it's supposed to be fun."

"Oh, forget it," I sigh. "I'll go see if there's any bacon left over for you."

Whiskers licks his lips. "Now that's what I'm talking about!"

* * * *

I push the front door open a crack and look right and left. The coast is clear. Whiskers follows me in, then shoots off toward my bedroom before anyone sees him. When I feel pretty sure he's safe, I turn toward the kitchen and *KA-BLAM!* My knee buckles and I'm on the floor again.

Tommy is wasting his time as a musician. If he focused half of his energy on harnessing his ninja skills instead of music that makes my eardrums bleed, he'd be unstoppable.

"Miss me, buddy?" he asks. He does something to my arm. It feels like he's setting me on fire with his bare hands. I hope that's not something they teach at scout camp.

"Not really," I cry.

He actually looks surprised that his torture isn't the best part of my day. "What'd you say?"

"No."

He twists the skin of my arm again and I yelp.

A horrible hissing noise comes from somewhere above my head. It grows louder and then mixes in with a low growl. I turn enough to see Whiskers a few feet away with his back arched and fur standing straight up.

"Buddy, your cat doesn't look very happy."

Whiskers stalks forward. "You're not gonna be happy if you don't—"

Tommy's face goes white and he tries to say something, but all that comes out is gibberish. To tell the truth, Scared Tommy isn't much different than Normal Tommy.

Mom comes out of the kitchen and stops when she sees us on the floor. Her eyes go from me to Tommy, then Whiskers, and back to me. "Boys, what are you doing?"

Tommy snaps out of being scared and grins. "Boys will be boys, am I right, Mom?"

"Get up! Both of you!" she cries. "And I've told you over and over, call me

Mrs. A. Heck, even call me Jane. But don't call me 'Mom.'"

Tommy's cheeks turn red as he scrambles to stand up.

Mom grabs one of my hands and helps me up. "Are you okay, Daniel?"

My knee hurts, but I shake my head.

She puts her hands on her hips. "Thomas, say you're sorry."

Tommy looks like he wants to tell her his name is Tommy, not Thomas, but he knows it would be a dumb move.

"Sorry, buddy."

"My name's Daniel, not buddy," I say.

He blinks but doesn't say anything. Then Mom makes him wait for Lila out on the porch.

"Now I want you to get that cat out of here. You know your sister's allergic." Mom turns back to face me.

"Cat? What cat?" I say. "Are you feeling okay, Mom? Maybe you caught what I had."

She spins around looking for Whiskers, who took off running as soon as Mom kicked Tommy out of the house. Then she rubs her eyes with her hands and says, "I need a nap. And chocolate."

* * * *

When I get back to my room I find Whiskers breathing heavy under my bed.

"Being real sure is hard, kid," he says.

"You're telling me." I plop down at my desk and stare at my notebook. "Thanks for sticking up for me out there. With Tommy."

One of my blankets fell off the bed this morning and Whiskers turns it into a cat bed. Before he closes his eyes, he yawns and shows me every one of his pointy teeth. "That's what friends do, right?"

"Yeah, I guess they do. Thank you for being my friend, Whiskers."

I wait for Whiskers to tell me what a great friend I am, but he doesn't say anything. When I look back, he's snoring.

* * * *

A little while later there's a knock on my door. Whiskers, who had been sunning himself on the edge of my desk, scrambles away so fast that he knocks my notebook onto the floor.

"Yeah?" I say as I bend over to pick it up.

Mom opens the door. Her hair stands up on one side of her head like she really did take a nap. "I'm sure you meant to say 'come in, best mother in the world,' didn't you?"

I shrug.

She stares at me from the doorway for a few seconds before coming over to sit on my bed. "No Annie today?" she asks.

"No."

"Is she not feeling well?"

I shrug again.

"Did something happen between you and Annie, Daniel?"

It's creepy how moms know almost everything without having to ask. My mom says it's "women's tuition" or something like that. I don't know what that means, but it sounds expensive.

Instead of answering her, I stare at the piece of paper in front of me. I don't want to tell her the truth because then she'll find out her handsome, witty, and amazing son isn't very nice. But when she looks into my eyes, I crumble.

"I wouldn't share my pen—*something* with her," I say.

She purses her lips. "I see."

Dad told me that Mom wanted to go to school to be one of those doctors who gets paid to listen to other people's problems. Instead of getting a fancy leather couch and a deeper understanding of brains and stuff, she got married and had Lila, and then me. Every once in a while she'll ask us how something makes us feel, and it's usually when I've gotten into big trouble and we're out of chocolate.

"I told her she was being greedy," I say.

"Hmm."

"But, really, I was the one being greedy. Because if she borrowed my—this *thing*, then I wouldn't have it to draw—to *do* stuff with."

Mom closes her eyes, and the corners of her mouth turn up a tiny bit. "How very specific of you."

I look at the floor. "Sorry."

She comes over to me and wraps her arms around my shoulders. "I'm so sorry you're hurting, honey. I know how much you care for Annie."

Tears blur my vision, and I bury my face in her shoulder. "I just miss her so much," I say.

"It's hard when someone you love is mad at you."

I shudder. Mom said the "L" word. It's bad enough to hear the kissy noises at school, but now Mom's getting in on it, too? "Love?" I sniff. "I don't love Annie. That's disgusting."

Mom rolls her eyes and ruffles my hair with her hand. "You *know* what I mean."

I won't admit it, but I do know what she means. "Do you think she'll ever forgive me?"

"Maybe. Or maybe not." She shrugs. "I don't know for sure, but the best you can do is say you're sorry and see."

My eyes wander back to the doodles on the page of my open notebook. Mom's given me an idea and I'm anxious to get started. "Thanks."

She smiles. "Of course, honey."

Before she leaves my room, I stop her. "Oh, and Mom?"

Her eyebrows raise. "Yes?"

"Do you think you could help me with something?"

"That depends," she says. "This wouldn't happen to involve a pogo stick, bottle rockets, or a badger, would it?"

My mom knows me so well. I laugh and shake my head. "Not this time. I want to know how to—how to make friends."

She smiles so big I can see almost every single one of her teeth. "You *really* want to know the secret to making friends, Daniel?"

"Yeah, I really do."

"You already know what to do."

"I do?"

Mom nods. "You do. Better than you realize."

And then she leaves me alone to think about what in the world she just said.

* * * *

I ride Lila's old pink bike, streamers and all, over to Annie's house. Her gift, a shiny silver toaster, sits in the front basket. It's not just any toaster—it's the UpandAt'Em-bot. This one spreads peanut butter on toast and ties shoelaces. Annie only knows how to tie her laces in bunny ears, so I figure the toaster is not only nutritious, but it's also educational. I tried to draw an invention that would make peanut butter AND jelly sandwiches that could also tie shoes, but it kept smearing jelly on my shoelaces and tying my bread. That design needs some more work.

I taped a note to the outside of the toaster, too. All it says is "I'm sorry," because I am sorry. It's not much, but Annie knows I'm not good with words.

Annie doesn't come to the door when I knock, but I know she's there.

She's kind of hard to miss because she's glaring out at me from her big living room window.

"Toast-er. For you." I mouth the words at her, pointing at the shiny square under my arm. I set it down on her doormat like I'm making an offering to the queen. I wait for a few minutes to see if she'll come out to grab her present, but she doesn't, so I leave.

When I ride my bike past her house fifteen minutes later, the toaster is gone. Someone who really likes toast could have snatched it from her doorstep, I guess, but when I try to talk to Annie at school on Monday her breath is extra peanut-buttery.

If only extra peanut-buttery meant we were still friends.

Chapter 9

Recess is boring when you don't have anyone to play with. Everyone else has someone, even Metal Mike who wears a helmet that looks like a cage so his teeth won't be crooked. Even Rain Stevens who eats seeds and leaves and talks to ghosts. Even Song Li, the new kid from China who knows like two words of English.

Not me. I don't have anyone. I have a notebook and a weird pencil.

Mom told me I know how to make friends. I want to believe her, but this is coming from the lady who tried to convince me to eat meatloaf by patting her belly and saying "mmm, so yummy." At this point, she's still regaining my trust.

I should be with Annie, playing kickball or pretending we're digging up dinosaur bones in the sandbox. Instead, I sit on the ground with my back against the bricks of the school building while she plays tag with a group on the jungle gym.

When I look up from my drawing, Annie stands in the far corner of the playground, surrounded by a group of fifth-graders. They're all yelling at her. Annie's hair hangs over her eyes and tears streak her cheeks.

I run as fast as I can to Annie's side. She won't look at me, but she grabs onto my arm with her hand, right where the bruises from Tommy are finally starting to heal. It doesn't hurt, though. I'm too angry to feel it.

"Oh, isn't that sweet? Your boyfriend's here." One of the boys laughs.

"We just lost the game because of her!" someone else whines.

A few others call Annie names. I can't listen to any more. Before anyone else can speak, I take a step toward the group.

"Leave her alone!" I growl, putting myself between Annie and the crowd.

"Or what?" Bucky Thomas asks, turning his head to spit. I think he spits on someone's face on accident, but they don't complain because they know it would be the last thing they do. Bucky is the biggest boy in the entire school. He already has to shave his beard every day, and I think he should add his knuckles to that list, too. Rumor has it that Bucky is really 26. No one's had the guts to ask if that's true or not.

"Or . . ." Or I don't know what.

So I do the first, and dumbest, thing I can think of. I pull the wood case from my pocket, grab the pencil, and start scribbling on my notepad.

"Awww, what's da widdle baby gonna do wiff him's widdle cwayon?" Bucky asks.

"Writing love notes to your *girllll-friend*?" someone else yells.

Before I can finish my drawing, Bucky pushes me, and I slam into the ground. The magic pencil goes flying and lands right in front of Annie's sneakers.

In the wrong hands, that pencil could mean the end of the world as we know it. I'm not afraid of Bucky finding and using the pencil, though. He can barely write his own name. Some of those other kids probably know how to draw, though, and I'm not so sure I want to know the kinds of things they imagine.

Annie walks away. I can't believe it. I stuck up for her, and she leaves without saying a thing. That hurts more than anything Bucky could do to me.

Bucky circles me like a prowling tiger. He laughs and kicks a cloud of wood chips over me. I cover my eyes with my hands.

This is the end, I tell myself. *And I had so much more I wanted to do with my life, too.*

"Bucky, stop!" a boy commands. I don't recognize his voice, and I'm too scared to look. Bucky might shoot more wood missiles towards my precious eyes and blind me forever. Or at least until he finishes me.

There's a lot of shuffling of feet, like there's a chase happening around the jungle gym. It lasts for a few minutes until someone falls down next to me with a cry and a thud. I'm afraid to open my eyes in case it's Bucky. A close-up image of that goon would be sure to haunt me in my nightmares.

"Not such a tough guy now, are ya?" Bucky sneers above me, not beside me. My heart pounds, now afraid that Annie's next to me in the dirt.

The kid next to me jumps up and runs off. Some of the other kids follow, but not Bucky. He's still close. The reek of his aftershave hangs over me like a rain cloud. A horrible, toxic, acid rain cloud. I curl my body up like an armadillo and wrap my hands around my head. Then I wait for him to attack.

"GET AWAY FROM MY FRIEND," Annie shouts, but it doesn't sound like Annie. Burning fire has replaced her cute squeak.

"Who's gonna make me?" Bucky sneers.

"I am," she says.

He laughs. "Oh, you are, are you? I'm reeeeeal scared."

Annie shrugs. "You don't have to be scared of me, I guess. But you should probably be scared of *him*."

It isn't until Bucky shrieks and runs away that I see the hole burned in the seat of his pants. The big kids forget all about us because they're too busy looking for cover from the half-bear, half-octopus floating in the sky.

"Daniel! Get up!" She grabs me by the arm and pulls me to my feet. We scramble to hide behind the climbing wall just as the beam of the wooden swing set splits in half and falls to the ground.

"So that's Octobear, huh?" Annie gasps.

"Yeah. He has laser beams in his eyeballs. Cool, right?"

Annie flashes her jack-o-lantern grin. "So cool."

I scratch my head. "I don't remember Octobear having a red bow on its head, though. Did you do that?"

"Maybe." She won't look at me.

I freeze in shock. First, it was Marcaroni. Now it's hair bows on my ferocious sea creature-stuffed animal mutant.

Annie's a girl. A real, live girl who secretly likes bows and the color pink. I don't believe it.

But now's not really the time to question everything I know about Annie, not with the playground crashing down around us. She saved me from the wrath of Bucky, that's what matters.

"I was really mean before, and I'm sorry," I say. "Thanks for helping me, Annie."

She kicks at a wood chip with her toe. "That's what friends do—help each other."

"Are we still friends?" I ask.

Off in the distance, Octobear roars an adorable roar and fires off his set of lasers.

"Of course we're still friends, Daniel," she says. "But it's okay to have other friends, too. I mean, look at all the friends you've made."

"What are you talking about?"

She nods toward the rest of the playground. "Take a look. They're all here. I mean, I drew a few of them for you, of course, but the others must have known you were in trouble and came to help."

"You drew them?"

Her cheeks turn pink. "I'm sorry that they're not very good, but I was trying to be fast."

I peek around the rock wall. She's right, they *are* all there. None of the drawings are perfect, their usual lines crooked or totally missing. It's okay, because none of us are perfect. All we can do is our best, even if our arms are crooked or we're missing one of our four eyes. If we're helping someone else, we're perfect. Each of Annie's messy drawings is exactly the way it should be.

Up ahead, the four-eyed aliens from the planet Beezo have a group of bullies pinned against the wall of the school. Their guns are out and pointed at the kids. The big one buzzes orders to the others. I do feel a little bad the kids are crying, but only a little. They're about to be bubbled, and that's all. When the smallest alien sees me, he waves his webbed hand. The big alien punches him in the arm.

On the far side of the yard, Sap has Bucky by the belt loops. The superhero is not pleased with the burn hole in his pants. Bucky's white as a sheet of paper, and all he does is holler when Sap asks him who he's working for.

Macaroni, the pink unicorn, munches on some grass on the other side of the schoolyard fence. I'm surprised Macaroni's here at all, but Annie shrugs. "He's still a unicorn. So what if he's purple and pink?"

A shadow passes over our heads and I look up as Herman, the blue dragon, makes a lazy loop in the sky. There's something on his back, something white and loud. "IIIIIIIIII HAAAAAAAATEEEEEEE FLLLLLLLYYYYYIIIIIINNNNNGGGG!" Whiskers screams. He digs his claws into Herman's neck to keep from shooting off into the air. Good thing Herman's skin is so thick.

Over by the Four Square court, Frog Squisher—I mean, Pat—Pratt stands next to Pi-zzabot. Pat's probably waiting for a pizza or help with his fractions homework or something. The sleeve of his shirt is ripped, and he keeps glancing in our direction.

"Did you know Pat distracted Bucky so I had enough time to draw everything?" Annie asks.

Pat Pratt helped me out. Pat Pratt, enemy to hopping creatures everywhere, risked receiving one of Bucky's hairy knuckles to the nose for me. I let this information roll around in my brain for a couple of seconds. "I'm going to see if Pat wants to take Herman for a ride," I announce.

Annie raises her eyebrow. "You are?"

I shrug. "Why not? He seems pretty okay, I guess . . . for a frog-squisher."

"Come on, Daniel. That happened in Second Grade." She shakes her head. "He is pretty okay. You guys might even turn out to be friends."

Friends. With someone besides Annie. I'm not sure what that means, but the idea doesn't scare me.

Octobear roars again and fires a laser right over our heads. Annie looks up and the red of the laser beams flashes in her eyes. "That's great and all, but we should probably keep that bear thing from destroying the school."

I nod and start to stand up.

Annie grabs my hand. "But one last thing."

She hands me a neatly-folded square of royal blue material. Black letters sewn to the fabric spell

"DANIEL." It's my very own cape. I grin and slip it over my shoulders. When I look over, Annie's putting on her cape, too.

Together we step out from behind the rock wall to save the day.

Love the Book?

If you enjoyed reading about Daniel and his crazy friends and want to read more, tell others!

One of the best ways to help my books reach more readers is by leaving a review or star rating on Amazon, Goodreads, or your own blog. If writing a review isn't your thing, even talking to a friend about DANIEL THE DRAW-ER helps a lot.

Thank you for supporting indie authors. You rock.

Go on Daniel's Next Adventure!

"No way." I cross my arms. "I'm not going."

Mom tries to hand me a brightly-colored Camp Bigfoot brochure, but I don't take it. If I take the brochure from her, she'll get the wrong idea. She'll think she actually has a chance of talking me into going. That's the first rule: never let the grown-ups see your weakness. If they sense you're weak, they'll pounce on you like a lion on a wildebeest. The next thing you know, you're wearing a frilly dress shirt and powder-blue bow tie to your Aunt Nancy's wedding and learning how to square dance. Do-si-*oh-no*.

At least, that's what *I've heard*.

"But look at how much fun these kids are having, Daniel." Mom points at a picture on the brochure. A kid around my age holds up a picture of a blobby animal made from macaroni glued to a piece of green construction paper.

"He's not really having fun," I say. "Fifth-graders don't like that kind of stuff. Only babies like making macaroni pictures."

"Then what about these kids on the water slide?" She points to another picture. "They're definitely having a blast."

I'm not impressed. "Eww. They're swimming in a lake. There's seaweed."

"So?"

"Seaweed is gross." My toes curl inside my sneakers just thinking about seaweed wrapping its long, slippery clutches around my poor, defenseless feet. *Yuck.*

She scrunches up her eyebrows and turns the paper over. Her eyes light up. "Here you go. The food looks good."

I lean close enough to tell she's lying. The glop of food on that boy's lunch tray looks like a hairball someone's cat coughed up. Mom's getting desperate, which means I have her right where I want her. "That's not food. I'd rather eat meatloaf for a whole month than whatever *that* is."

I'd rather chow down on a cardboard box sprinkled with paper clips than eat my mom's meatloaf, so promising to eat it at all is a pretty big deal.

Mom slaps the brochure down on the table and covers her face with her hands. "Why are you being so impossible?"

"I'm not being impossible. I like being home." I flutter my eyelashes at her. "With you, *best mommy in the whole world.*"

Even though she smiles back at me, I know she's not buying it. "Summer camp is fun, Daniel. You'd like it, if only you'd give it a chance."

I don't want to give it a chance. I want to spend my summer at home. Here, I have my own bed and a bathroom I only have to share with my older sister, Lila. Lila's always in the bathroom messing with her hair or putting on her war paint, but if I dance around and act like I'm going to accidentally pee on the floor, she rolls her eyes and leaves.

When I'm home, I don't have to worry about getting picked on by the older kids. Most of them leave me alone now, but Bucky Thomas still hasn't let me forget about the playground incident. Bucky's the biggest kid in my school and has to be about twenty-five years old now, but I'm pretty sure I heard him say he was going to be at camp this summer.

And, best of all, the bug-to-Daniel ratio is pretty even here.

Bugs. *Yeeeesh*.

What can I say? I like being home. This place is my castle, and castles are totally awesome.

"Going to Camp Bigfoot is a family tradition." A goofy grin spreads across Mom's face. "That's where your dad and I met. Look how well that turned out."

I sneak a chocolate chip cookie from the cookie jar while she's distracted by her lovey-dovey, kissy-wissy memories. "Gross," I mumble through a bite of chocolatey goodness. "One more reason not to go to camp. Girls."

"Even Annie's going," Mom adds, watching my reaction. "I talked to her mom this morning."

"Good for her." I sip my milk, hiding the panic flashing through me.

I don't believe it. The last time my best friend, Annie, mentioned summer plans, all she talked about was their family trip to the Grand Canyon and how she wanted to throw one of my plastic parachute men over the cliff. She never once mentioned camp.

Our friend Frog-Squisher—I mean, *Pat*—Pratt told me his parents signed him up for camp months ago. Without

Pat and Annie, I'll be all alone here for an entire week.

"I hope you like to get dirty, because if you stay home I'm puttin' you to work. This house is a disaster."

The last time Mom called the house a disaster, she made me clean all of the bathrooms. By myself. With a toothbrush. *Yuck.*

Baby craft projects, icky seaweed, and science experiment meals; or a week of crusty loaf-shaped meat, reruns on TV, and probably helping my mom weed the flower beds and scrub toilets? It's a tough choice, but she's going to have to try harder than that.

"Hmm." Mom flips through her calendar. "Looks like I have appointments set up for that week already. Maybe Miss Reznick can babysit when I volunteer at the clinic on

Tuesday. Oh, and again on Thursday when I have to—"

Miss Reznick lives next door, by herself—unless you count her thirty cats. I always see her in the grocery store wearing a string of pearls, her old bathrobe, and a pair of combat boots. The last time Miss Reznick stopped by for a visit, she pinched my cheeks so hard she left dents. Mom's never asked her to babysit before, but I don't put anything past someone who sees no problem poisoning her family with meatloaf.

"Fine. I'll go." The words slip from my mouth before I can stop them.

Mom squeals. She's on the phone with the camp before I can take it back. I'm not sure why she's so excited to get rid of me, but something tells me it involves sleeping in and not having to explain to the school principal why her son's Octobear destroyed half of the playground.

My mouth drops open when I realize what I've just done. Bubbles gurgle in my stomach and I set down my half-eaten cookie. I'm not hungry anymore, not even for chocolate chip cookies.

I can't believe Mom tricked me so easily. She's a worthy opponent.

As if I wasn't feeling bad enough already, my older sister Lila flounces into the kitchen and heads toward the refrigerator.

"Lila, honey," Mom's eyes twinkle. "Guess who's going to camp with you?"

I close my eyes and groan. I'd forgotten about Lila. Every summer, she works at Camp Bigfoot, though I have no idea what she does there. All she's really good at is doing her hair and bossing me around. Not only will I have to watch out for Bucky and stinky seaweed and spiders, but now I've got to keep away from my sister, too. This just keeps getting better.

Lila grabs a stalk of celery from the vegetable drawer and slams the refrigerator door. My sister says she likes celery because it tastes good, but I don't believe her for one second. No one eats celery because they like it, and I know for a fact it tastes like grass. She only eats it around me because she knows the sound of her gnawing drives me nuts.

Lila glares at me and sinks her teeth into her snack.

Crunch-crunch-crunch.

"Mo-om! Tell me he's not taking that ridiculous cape."

Crunch-crunch.

"Hey!" I wrap my arms around my chest, pulling my cape tight against my body. "I think the word you're looking for is 'cool.'"

Crunch.

She points the rest of her celery stalk at me. "Actually, the word I'm looking for, I can't say in front of Mom."

Crunch-crunch-crunch-crunch.

"Well, the word I'm looking for is so awful they haven't even invented it yet." I stick out my tongue at her. Annie made this cape just for me. I can't help it if my sister's jealous because none of her boring friends made her a cape.

"Enough, you two." Mom pinches the bridge of her nose between her fingers and sighs. "If you both don't cut it out I'll—"

"Make Lila give me her allowance?" I offer.

"Make *someone else* babysit Daniel for an entire week at Camp Bigfoot?" Lila rolls her eyes. She makes sure Mom can't see it or it'll be the last thing her precious eyeballs do.

"Just go," Mom groans. The last thing I hear from her before I leave is something about there not being enough chocolate in this world.

* * * *

Up in my room, I plop down at my desk and stare out the window. Usually, I sit and work on my drawings, but there's no way I can concentrate. I've never been away from home for more than a night, and now my parents want to send me away for almost a whole week to a wilderness crawling with spiders and centipedes. That should be no big deal for Annie. My best friend loves all kinds of insects, the creepy-crawlier the better. She even slurped down an entire earthworm when we were in kindergarten. I don't feel the same way about bugs and worms and mosquitoes. Don't even get me started on bees.

Bees!

I'm breathing heavy and little stars dance behind my eyelids as I think of all of the evil bees I've met during my life. Their angry buzzing, the glint of light off their stinger, the way they chase you until you cry for your mom . . .

My cat, Whiskers, jumps up to the edge of my desk. "Have you finished drawing the Bacon-bot 2000 yet?" He pats his fluffy white belly with a paw. "I'm wasting away to nothing, here."

Some people might be scared of a talking cat, but not me. Ever since I started using the magic pencil I found in the attic, my drawings have come to life—even my drawing of a blabbermouth cat named Whiskers.

In other words, my life has been pretty strange lately.

When I don't answer him, Whiskers places his paw on my notebook paper. "You okay, kid?"

"No," I say. "I'm not okay. My life is ruined."

My life is worse than ruined. I'm going to camp.

* * * *

Want to know what happens to Daniel and his friends at Camp Bigfoot?

Buy DANIEL THE CAMP-ER, Book 2 in the DANIEL THE DRAW-ER series today!

About the Author

S. J. Henderson is the author of the children's books DANIEL THE DRAW-ER and DANIEL THE CAMP-ER, as well as the Young Adult novel IN THE MIDDLE

S. J. lives in Michigan with her husband and four wild boys. When she is not writing about talking cats and pizza-baking robots, S. J. can usually be found riding one of her family's horses or drinking a little bit of coffee with her creamer.

Visit S. J.'s website:
www.sjhenderson.net

Follow S. J. on Twitter:
@SunnyJHenderson

Follow S. J. on Facebook:
www.facebook.com/authorsunnyhenderson

Made in the USA
Lexington, KY
26 February 2017